This book belongs to:

_____

_____

_____

First published by Walker Books Ltd.,
87 Vauxhall Walk, London SE11 5HJ

First U.S. paperback edition 2009

Library of Congress Cataloging-in-Publication Data is available.

Library of Congress Catalog Card Number 2003055653

ISBN 978-0-7636-2369-2 (hardcover)
ISBN 978-0-7636-4368-3 (paperback)

17 18 19 20 APS 10

Printed in Humen, Dongguan, China

This book was typeset in Lucy Cousins.
The illustrations were done in gouache.

Candlewick Press
99 Dover Street
Somerville, Massachusetts 02144

visit us at www.candlewick.com

Maisy
Goes Camping

Lucy Cousins

CANDLEWICK PRESS

One day,
Maisy decided
to go camping.

And all
her friends
came along.

They found the
perfect place to
make a camp.

Pitching a tent is not easy!

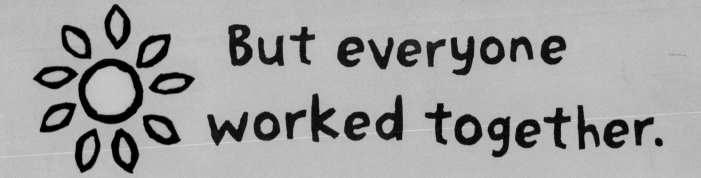

But everyone
worked together.

Oh no! The tent fell down!
So they tried again...

and again...until the
tent stayed up.

Good job, everyone!

That night, they sang around the campfire. Then it was time for bed.

Cyril went in first
with his flashlight.

One in
the
tent!

Next came Charley.
Watch the pegs!

Two in
the tent!

Then it was Tallulah's turn.
Three in the tent!

Make room for Maisy!
Four in the tent!

Is there
room for
one more?
Come on,
Eddie!

Oh no!
Five in the...
What a
squash!

What a
squeeze!

What a squeezy squish-squash!

Five in
the tent!

Good night,
campers!

POP!
Out came
Cyril.

POP!

Out
came
Tallulah.

POP!

Out came Charley.

POP!

Out came Maisy.

One in the tent,
four under the stars.
Sleep tight, campers!

Hoot! Hoot!